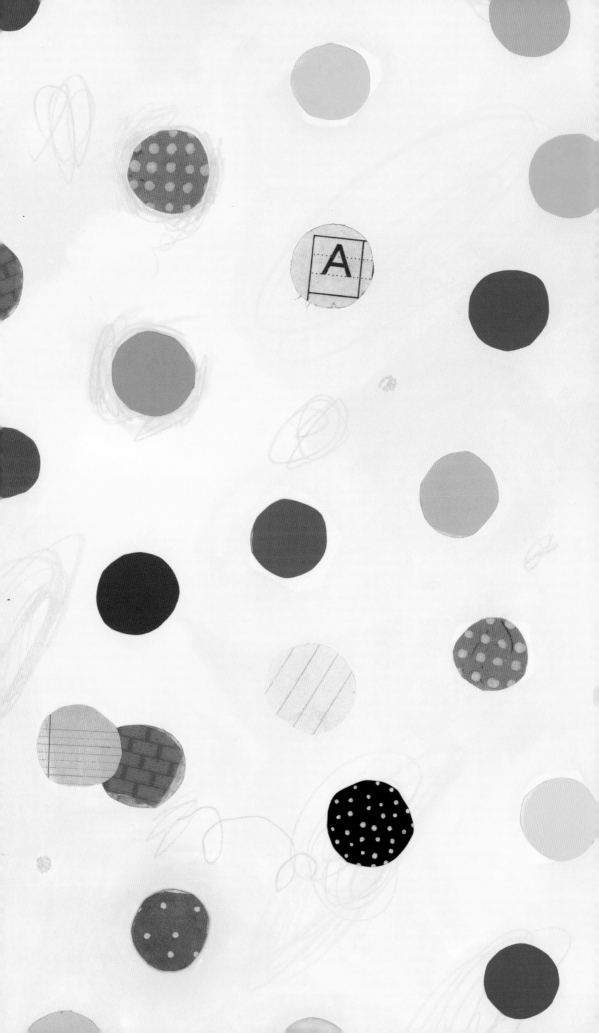

Giggle-Wiggle Wake-Up!

BY NANCY WHITE CARLSTROM

ILLUSTRATED BY MELISSA SWEET

ALFRED A. KNOPF
NEW YORK

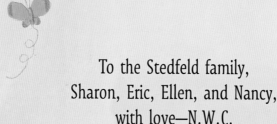

To the Stedfeld family,
Sharon, Eric, Ellen, and Nancy,
with love—N.W.C.

To Azalea Moon—M.S.

THIS IS A BORZOI BOOK PUBLISHED BY ALFRED A. KNOPF

Text copyright © 2003 by Nancy White Carlstrom.
Illustrations copyright © 2003 by Melissa Sweet.
All rights reserved under International and Pan-American Copyright Conventions.
Published in the United States by Alfred A. Knopf, an imprint of Random House Children's Books,
a division of Random House, Inc., New York, and simultaneously in Canada
by Random House of Canada Limited, Toronto. Distributed by Random House, Inc., New York.
KNOPF, BORZOI BOOKS, and the colophon are registered trademarks of Random House, Inc.
www.randomhouse.com/kids

Library of Congress Cataloging-in-Publication Data
Carlstrom, Nancy White.
Giggle-Wiggle wake-up! / by Nancy White Carlstrom ; illustrated by Melissa Sweet.
p. cm.
SUMMARY: Sammy wakes up to Monday morning sunshine, has breakfast, and heads to preschool.
ISBN 0-375-81350-0 (trade) — ISBN 0-375-91350-5 (lib. bdg.)
[1. Morning—Fiction. 2. Nursery schools—Fiction. 3. Schools—Fiction. 4. Stories in rhyme.] I. Sweet, Melissa, ill. II. Title
PZ8.3.G1948Gi 2003   [E]—dc21   2002043320
Manufactured in China
October 2003
10 9 8 7 6 5 4 3 2 1
First Edition

Sunlight, fun light
Skipping through the window
Sunlight, fun light
Warm on Sammy's bed
Swirl in, twirl in
Monday morning sunshine
T i n y   S h i n y
Warms a sleepyhead
It's a tiny-shiny wake-up
It's a tiny-shiny day

Scrit scrat, scrit scrat
Nudging the door open
Pit pat, kit cat
Round and round she goes
  Creep in, leap in
  Monday morning kitten
  Fur thick, purr lick
  Tickle Sammy's toes

It's a tickle-lickle leap-up
It's a tickle-lickle day

Sniff snuff, sniff snuff
Smells come from the kitchen
S i z z l e D r i z z l e
Working like a clock
Sniffed in, whiffed in
Monday morning breakfast
Lips smack, snick snack
Sammy's tummy talks

It's a sniffy-whiffy eat-up
It's a sniffy-whiffy day

Slide in, hide in
Playing in the bedroom
Sammy, nowhere
Nothing but a box

Sides shake, noise make
Monday morning silly
Peek out, squeak out
Silly-willy squawks

It's a silly-willy pop-up
It's a silly-willy day

Wash face, wash face
Splashing with cold water
Brush teeth, brush teeth
Flash a smiley face
   Dressing, combing
   Monday morning Sammy
   All done, Sam won
   The getting-ready race

It's a splashy-flashy wash-up
It's a splashy-flashy day

Bing bang, bing bang
Busy whizzy wildness
Cling clang, cling clang
Rattle from the street
Beep on, sweep on
Monday morning loudness
Whizz zoom, bizz boom
Cars and trucks and feet

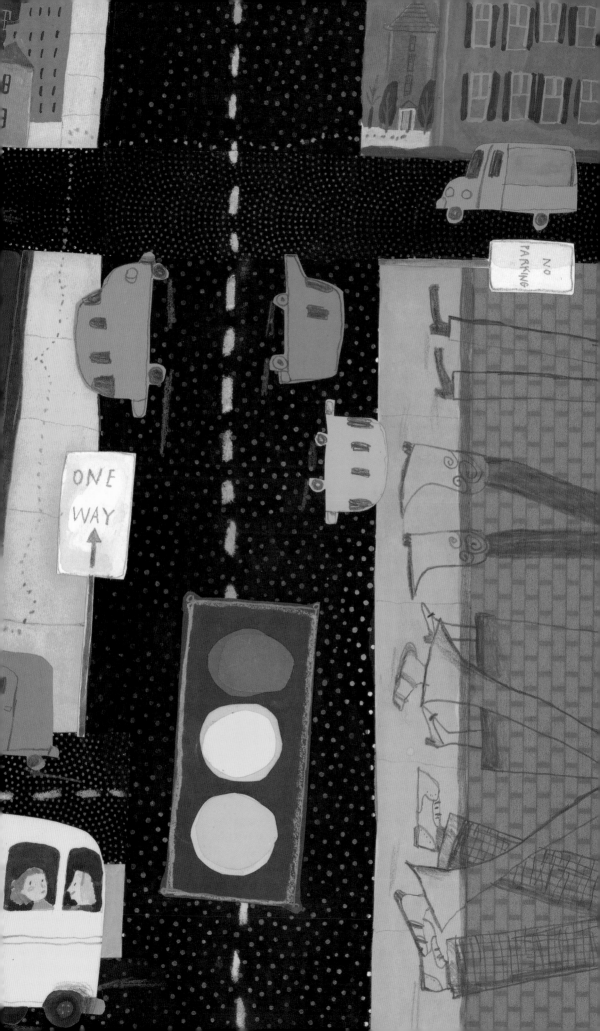

It's a whizzy-tizzy speed-up
It's a whizzy-tizzy day

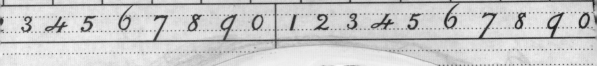

Tiptoe, tiptoe
Quietly she's walking
Bending, down low
Getting very near

123

Miss me, kiss me
Monday morning Mama
Love you, love you
Soft in Sammy's ear

It's a love-you-so-much snuggle-up
It's a love-you-so-much day

Clomp-stomp, clomp-stomp
Noisily we're marching
Clashing, click-sticks
Pounding on the drum
Sing it, ring it
Monday morning music
Play it, say it
With a toot and hum

It's a jingle-jangle juggle-up
It's a jingle-jangle day

Klunk-thunk, klunk-thunk
Building a high tower
F u z z y W u z z y
Rabbit on the run

Snatch it, catch it
Monday morning children
Falling over
Tipsy-topsy fun

It's a giggle-wiggle jump-up
It's a giggle-wiggle day!

It's a tiny-shiny wake-up

and a tickle-lickle leap-up

and a sniffy-whiffy eat-up—

don't you know?

It's a silly-willy pop-up

and a splashy-flashy wash-up

and a whizzy-tizzy speed-up—

here we go!

It's a love-you-so-much snuggle-up

and a jingle-jangle juggle-up.

It's a giggle-wiggle jump-up . . .

It's a giggle-wiggle day!

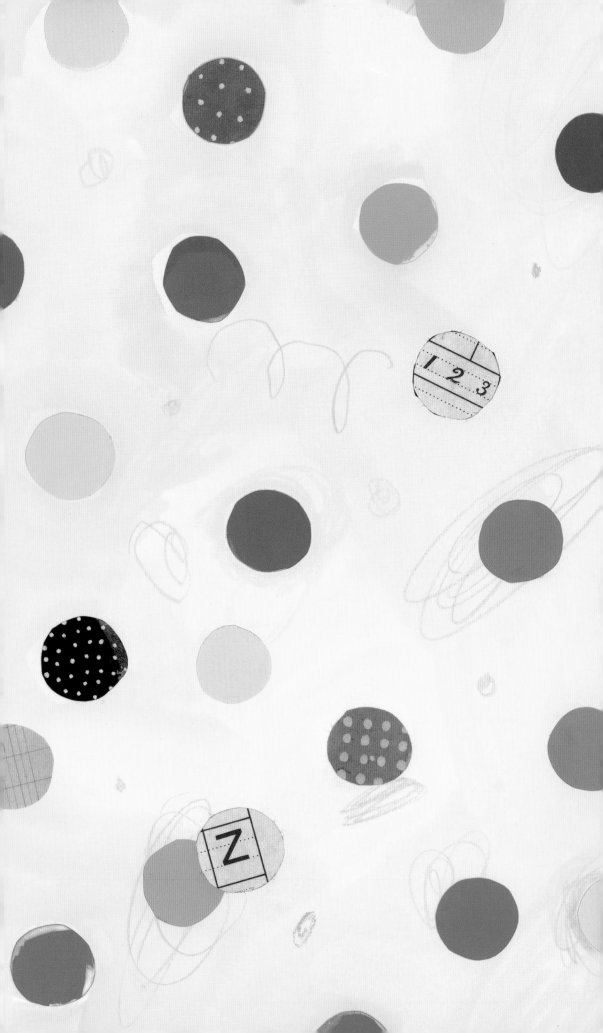